Dedication

To my husband, Ed, my parents, Vincent and Doris, my sisters, Lisa and Michele, and my friends, Ida, Mindy, Theresa, Wanda, and Christie. Thank you for your love, help, and support!

Thank you to my synchro coaches, Barbara, Donna, and Dale. Without your dedication to synchronized swimming, I would not have this wonderful sport in my life!

Thank you to Australian swimmer, Annette Kellermann (1887-1975), who popularized synchronized swimming for women!

Dear Parents,

Do you have a daughter who loves swimming? Is she the child you can't get out of the pool to have lunch or put more lotion on? Does she also like to dance, listen to music, or play dress up? If any of these things apply, you might have a "Water Ballerina" or "Synchronized Swimmer" on your hands!

I first learned synchronized swimming at a swim club in Staten Island, NY when I was eleven years old. After six summers of swimming at the club, I competed for four years with the synchronized swim team at Hunter College in Manhattan. Now I am on the Gotham Synchronized Swim Team in Manhattan and compete with this team at the "U.S. Masters Synchronized Swimming National Championships".

My reason for writing this book is to spread awareness of this wonderful sport to young children. It is a great way to stay physically fit and is creatively rewarding. Swimmers choose their own music, choreograph their own routines, and wear matching swimsuits. Clubs or teams usually put on "water shows" and compete in regional and national age group competitions.

I hope you and your child enjoy reading my story and become curious about this sport. The best way to find "Synchronized Swimming" groups or teams is to inquire at your local YMCA, swim clubs, and summer camps, or go online to: www.usasynchro.org and click on "membership" to locate one close to your hometown.

Swimmingly yours,

Diane Garcia

Hi! My name is Wendy Willow and I'm going to tell you how I became a *Water Ballerina*. Water ballerinas are also called *Synchronized* Swimmers*.

*synchronized (sing-kruh-nahyzd)

It all begin when I was eleven years old. I lived in a nice house with my mom, dad, and two sisters. Lisa, the oldest, was sixteen, Michele, the youngest, was six, and I was the middle sister.

Here is my story...

3

One Saturday afternoon my dad said, "Hey Wendy, do you want to go see the swim club we're joining this summer?" I said, "Sure dad," and hopped in the car.

As we drove, my dad told me the club was still under construction and we were just going to take a look. I was so happy to be going with my dad on this adventure.

When we got there, we saw a huge
pool, some buildings, and lots
of mud. As we made our way to
the pool deck, I could feel myself
begin to tingle with excitement.

A friendly man came over to us. He was
one of the owners and introduced me to his
daughter, Nancy. While our fathers talked, we
started playing and got to know each other.

After a while, Mr. Johnson, the owner, invited us to look at the building plans. On the plans I noticed a stage, with a large shell behind it, and a dance floor. I asked Mr. Johnson about it and he said it was a band shell where the orchestra would be playing during the Saturday night dances.

That night, as I lay in bed, I started thinking about my day. I was very excited about the summer ahead and the new friend I made. I started thinking about the band shell and all the people dancing under the stars, as I drifted off to sleep.

Before I knew it, my sisters and I finished the school year, and it was time to begin our first summer at the swim club!

We were the happiest children on the planet! We would leave the house at 8:30 each morning and get home about 7:00 at night. By the time we returned home, we were exhausted, but very happy!

One afternoon during our first summer, Barbara, one of the lifeguards, was starting a synchronized swimming class. I had never heard of this before, and was shy about joining. She saw that I was scared and waved me over. I was so glad she did because it CHANGED MY LIFE FOREVER!

Synchronized swimming is like ballet* in the water! The swimmers move together in patterns to music. They perform figures, like ballet legs and dolphins, and hear the music both above and below the water. The music is heard underwater through a special waterproof speaker. Swimmers choose their own music, write their own routines, and wear matching swimsuits and headpieces with glitter.

*ballet (ba-lay)

That summer was like a dream! We met so many families just like ours. We even went on cloudy days if I had Synchro practice.

I became friends with Kathy. She was on the Synchro Team too. We spent hours in the pool practicing, along with my younger sister, Michele, and her friend, Tina.

13

As the summer went on, our friendships grew and our synchro skills got better. There were now about fifteen girls on the team.

One day, Barbara, our synchro coach, gathered us together and told us we would be putting on a Water Show at the end of the summer.

We were filled with anticipation! We had so much to do! Barbara spoke to us about choosing music, routines, and our costumes. She would sew some of the costumes, but would need help. Michele and I immediately volunteered our mom.

As the days went by, the program for the Water Show began to come together. My group would swim to the song "Raindrops Keep Falling On My Head".

The Marvelous Collection of Alvin Guilbert

A Mermendium Story

...

By Manelle Oliphant

A Note From the Author

My Dear Friends,

Thanks so much for your response to this project. It marks the third mermendium book, and I appreciate your support as I've created it.

Because I wanted the book to look handmade I scanned the painted sketchbook pages with tape and paper clips attached. So, there could be issues with print quality, like odd margins and shadows in the gutter. I kept it this way to try and give you the experience of holding the imperfect original version in your hands.

The same idea applied to the text. Because I hand wrote everything there are bound to be mistakes that a computer would have caught. I hope, when you find them you'll enjoy them as another quirky part of the book.

Thank you all,

Manelle Oliphant

THE MARVELOUS COLLECTION OF ALVIN GUILBERT

AN INTERVIEW BY MANELLE OLIPHANT

DON'T DISTURB THE MERMAIDS!

Striped Large Mouth Tiny Specimen 12 cm.

Mr. Alvin Guilbert

An interview with Mr. Alvin Guilbert, conducted by Manelle Oliphant. Lake Semipuella, MT, May 1, 1937

I met Mr. Guilbert in his now barren laboratory. His large desk loomed in the room's center covered in notes and papers much as I imagined it always had. But the walls and shelves, where there had once been a magnificent collection of mermaid specimens, were empty.

I smiled at Mr. Guilbert across the messy desk. "I'm grateful for the chance to conduct this interview."

Guilbert, a bony man with wild hair, shrugged. I soon learned this is one of his signature gestures. "I think it's time people learned what really happened, instead of the version printed in the papers."

I don't think his modesty was an act. He may have saved the world, but it hasn't gone to his head. "Tell us about yourself, Mr. Guilbert."

He shrugged again. "I grew up here near Lake Semipuella." He points out the window toward the lake. Green moss covered beaches where only weeks ago everything was brown and dying. "That means I should've known better. Everyone here lives by one rule. Don't disturb the mermaids." He sighed. "I did though and almost killed them all

2.

1.

3.

Specimen 1.
spotted small mouth
28 inches
found July 1922

Specimen 2.
slimy merm
12 inches
found Nov. 1922

Specimen 3.
small blue
14 inches
found January 1923
frozen.

George, Pearl and Alvin 1922

I paused unsure if I should ask my next question. "If you knew better why did you do it?"

"It was the day George died. He was my best friend, him and Pearl." Guilbert's voice grew quieter as he talked, the pain of loss and betrayal etched on his face. "When we were 13 the three of us went fishing. A storm blew in and our boat hit something, we were thrown overboard." Mr. Guilbert paused and took a deep breath before continuing. "I saw George struggling in the water. His life jacket had come off. I tried to save him but I couldn't."

Guilbert stood up and walked over to a space on the shelf. I can see a circle where lack of dust told me something used to sit there. "What we hit was a mermaid. I found her dead on the beach after it was all over. She became the first specimen in my collection. She sat right here for over fifteen years." He put his hand on the shelf. "I used to look at her and think that even though I couldn't save George I could make his death count by saving mermaids like her. I didn't know then that my keeping her perpetuated the problem."

MERMAIDS OF LAKE SEMIPUELLA

SUCKER

MINIS
BROWN

SMALL MOUTH

SLIMY MERM

LONG

GREEN

SMALL
BLUE

LARGE MOUTH

GIANT NAIAD

LARGE BLUE   EEL MERM

Your other friend, Pearl Harvey, survived, didn't she? She became your partner?"

Guilbert turned toward me. "Eventually. George's death devastated her. When she started to heal she began to come over and help me. The science didn't interest her much, but she kept things organized."

He sat down and shuffled the papers on his desk as if he'd just noticed they were out of order. When he finished, they looked much as they had before. "For years Pearl and I worked together. If I had an idea, I'd run it by her first. She had a way of helping me turn them into reality. But, she often talked of leaving. Maybe she saw our work as her ticket to a different life, a way of burying George. But I didn't listen. I thought we'd work together until we were old and gray. She was the first to support my idea that we needed to study the moss as well as the mermaids."

Large Longs
large longs grow from 25" to 45" and their colors usually range from yellow-green to blue green

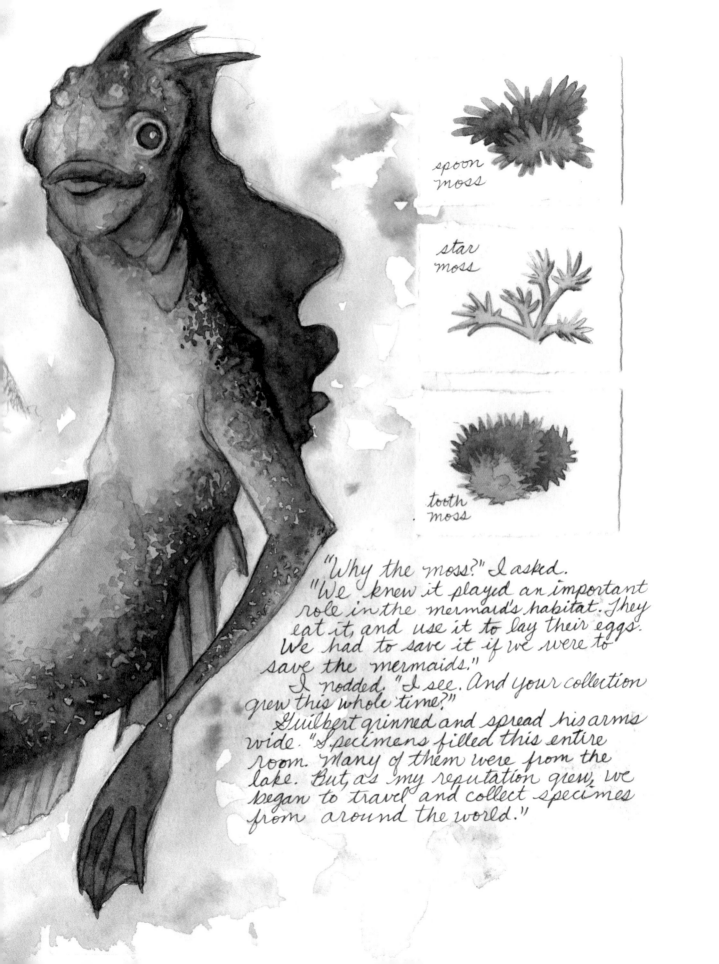

spoon
moss

star
moss

tooth
moss

"Why the moss?" I asked.
"We knew it played an important role in the mermaid's habitat. They eat it, and use it to lay their eggs. We had to save it if we were to save the mermaids."

I nodded. "I see. And your collection grew this whole time?"

Guilbert grinned and spread his arms wide. "Specimens filled this entire room. Many of them were from the lake. But, as my reputation grew, we began to travel and collect specimens from around the world."

"And how did you get into contact with Professor Foley?" I asked. "As I understand it, your work with him is what led to your discovery."

Professor Foley ran an ad in a scientific magazine. Pearl and I had been waiting for such an opportunity. Guilbert opened a desk drawer rummaged around and pulled out a cutting from a magazine.

SAVE ME

$10,000 Grant
Help Save the Mermaids!

NAIADOLOGIST, PROF. FOLEY, IS LOOKING FOR A RESEARCH TEAM.

The chosen team will travel to the professor's laboratory on the shores of Lake Nymphette. Have access to all his research and grant money to continue naiadology research. All qualified candidates should apply.

WRITE TO:
SAVE THE MERMAIDS, 45 LAKE ROAD, LAKE NYMPHETTE, TEXAS

MINI: GREEN 20"

MINI: BROWN 8" Collected 3 April '23

"So you applied and got the grant?"

Guilbert nodded, "That's right."

"How was it that the professor had so much money?"

"You know I had the same question. I don't think Professor Foley is a professor. He's well educated, but that's as far as it goes. I think he's called the professor because he wants to be. He's rich, family money, so people do what he wants."

I leaned forward "What happened after you got the grant?"

"We traveled to Lake Nymphette and started our research." Guilbert paused here and grimaced. "I said 'our research', but I didn't see much of Pearl after that. Professor Foley made her the official face of the operation. She would check in on my progress and report it to the press. They were very interested in what we were doing. Marketing was Prosefsor Foley's forte. Pearl's too apparently

Lake Nymphette

Pearl Harvey and Alvin Guilbert

MERWORM
14" Collected 16 Jun '32

"What did you think of the professor?"

Guilbert shrugged. "The first time I met him he wore a white three piece suit. He was the type to blow his nose on dollar bills. Not at all professorish."

I nodded. "How was working with him?"

"The lab was state of the art, and his collection of specimens was greater than mine. He was enthusiastic about all my ideas. If I ever needed equipment or anything else, he made sure I got it. There were no budget restraints or delays. Those parts were nice."

"But other parts weren't?"

Guilbert shrugged again. "I think I mostly missed Pearl. She used to be there to bounce ideas off of, but after we moved she was always out. I'd like to say I had an inkling of what she was doing, but I didn't. Even with the construction by the lake and Pearl's comments I didn't suspect.

"What comments were those?"

"She often mentioned plans for the amusement park." Guilbert spoke in a high pitched voice. "You know Alvin, she'd say, 'you don't need to try so hard. There are lots of exciting things on the horizon.'"

I laughed at his impression. "Tell me about the amusement park."

"The professor planned to open a mermaid-themed holiday destination. He gave me the false idea it would be a living museum, with rides. They were building it near the lab."

"When did you learn he was lying?"

"Later on, when they left me in the middle of the country."

"After you tried to move the mermaids, you mean?"

"Yes, after that."

carrot
mermaids
native to
Lake Nymphette

Professor Foley

I tapped my pen to my chin. "Moving the mermaids couldn't have been your first course of action, it seems rather drastic."

"Your right. I worked for months before we came up with that plan. I tested the water, trying to understand why the moss was dying. I made sure the lab and construction site weren't contaminating anything. I added new minerals to the water and transplanted live moss to areas where the moss had died. Nothing worked, and the mermaid population kept diminishing."

"Is that when you decided to move them?"

"Not yet. There were a lot of other measures we tried. It's a long list. I wanted so much to save them. I thought I could control their decline if I just tried one more thing, studied one more specimen. Finally we estimated Lake Nymphette's population to be under a hundred living mermaids. It used to have thousands. That's when we decided to move them."

"It must have been a lot of work?"

Guilbert leaned back on his chair. "We planned for weeks. We had to find trucks with tanks large enough to transport the

specimens. Then modify them
with environmental controls."
    I thought back to the reports
I'd read detailing the vast operation.
"We read a lot about these
preparations in the papers. How
did you feel about the attention
the project got from the press?"
    Guilbert took a deep breath. "The
professor and Pearl insisted it
would help our cause. I didn't
read most of the articles, found
them distracting. That turned out
to be a mistake."
    "Why?"
    "When I read the reports later I
learned they'd misrepresented
what was happening."

MINI: Sucker Merm
10 inches April 7, 1934

MINI: Violet
6 inches August 18, 1935

MINI: Long
14 inches July 29, 1933

*spiney merm
native of
Lake Nymphette*

spiney fish

sucker fish

Mer-transport tanker

"I read your trip with the mermaids started out bad and got worse. That's not what happened."

Guilbert shook his head. "Not at all. Things went well. I knew all the mermaids wouldn't survive the trip, but it surprised me how many seemed to be thriving. When I cleaned the tanks each day there were only a few unlucky specimens."

"You mean dead?"

"Yes, The deaths were much less than what I calculated. And then there was the moss."

I blinked at him. "What about it?"

"The same moss that grew on the lake shores grew in the tanks whenever I fished out the mermaids' dead bodies."

I grimaced. It sounded like dirty work. "That was unusual?"

"Only because I didn't understand how it got there."

"A mystery?"

Guilbert smiled. "Yes."

"So the mermaids did well. When did you find out the papers reported something different?"

"Oh, it was after I was abandoned, I suppose."

I blinked. "Abandoned?"
"Yes, the whole expedition left me behind. I woke up one day to an empty parking lot and a note from Pearl. She said they didn't think the mermaids would make it and the professor thought it best to take them home."
"How did that make you feel?"
"I didn't understand why the professor hadn't consulted me. But, things began to make sense on my ride home."

flubmer

Mershark

Wolfmer

"How did you get home?"
"The professor left me his car
and driver. It happened that
there were weeks worth of newspapers
left on the back seat. "That's
when I read what they'd been
saying about the expedition."
"The articles were enough for you
to figure out the professor's
real plans?"
"The articles, the advertisement,
and the things Pearl had said."
"What advertisement?" I asked.

Merpup

Merperch

Catfish Mermaid

"It was an advertisment for the amusment park. Let me see if I still have a copy."

He rummaged in his desk and pulled out a copy of a news paper dated a few weeks ago. He opened to a page in the middle and pointed to an ad, and scowled. "You see, they planned to display the mermaid specimens from the professor's collection in some kind of horror show. Keeping the mermaids alive didn't matter one jot. It was disgusting."

Tench Mer native to Lake Nymphette

"If it didn't matter that they were alive why hire you?"

"Publicity. He wanted to be seen as a hero." Guilbert slumped into his seat. "I learned later the professor thought I was most likely to kill off the mermaids. thats why he chose us for the grant."

I blinked in surprise. "It was all a ruse? Was Pearl on his side from the beginning?"

"I have no idea when he turned Pearl. Part of me wishes we never applied for that grant. But, I wouldn't have been able to save the mermaids without it."

"Tell me what you did next."

"When I got home, I came and sat down right here." He tapped his chair. "I was so... I'd trusted Pearl, and she'd..." He trailed off.

"Betrayed you?" I supplied.

"Yes, she'd betrayed me. I thought she was my best friend." He paused and took a deep breath.

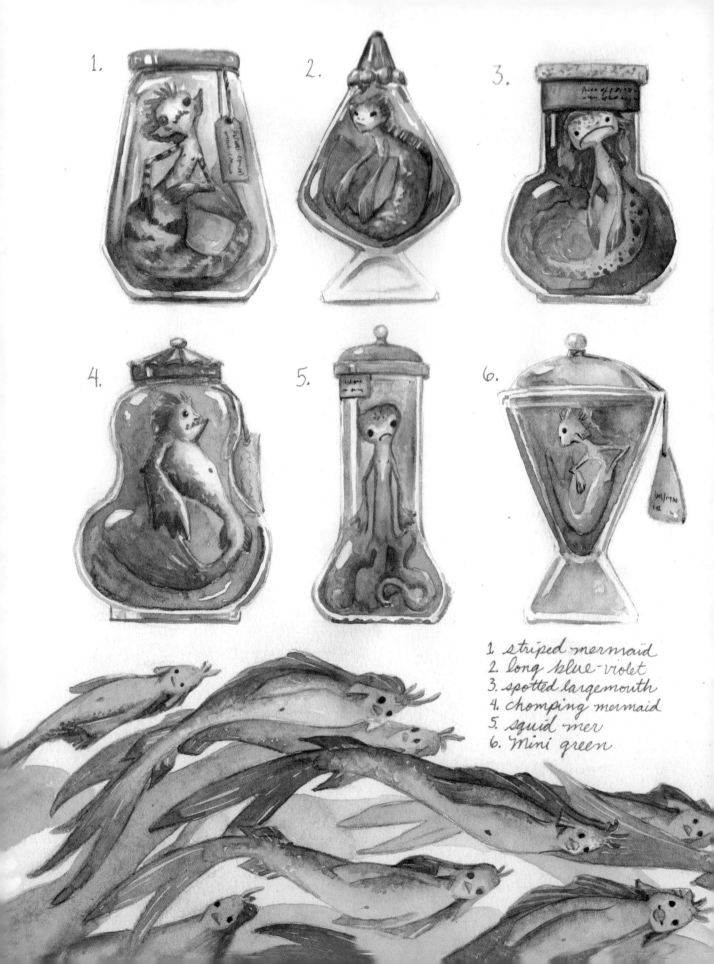

1. striped mermaid
2. long blue-violet
3. spotted largemouth
4. chomping mermaid
5. squid mer
6. mini green

"Why do you think she did it?" I asked.

"Oh, I'm sure there were many reasons. The professor paid her a great deal, and the fantastic lifestyle he offered was tempting as well. It's much more glamorous than life here." Guilbert stopped talking and glanced toward the window. "I sat here staring at a collection of dead mermaids. For years I told myself each specimen was there to study. Each one helped save it's kindred. But, I realized it wasn't true. Pearl had betrayed me, and I'd betrayed the mermaids."

I gazed around at the empty shelves "How's that?"

"All my efforts had only made things worse." He stood up from his chair again and walked to the same empty spot he'd pointed out earlier "I came here, to this shelf, and hefted my first mermaid into my arms." He pantomimed picking up a heavy object. "She was a larger specimen, 28 inches, and preserved in formaldehyde. I took her out to the exact place I'd found her."

He waved me over. I got up from my seat and followed him outside "Right here." He pointed at the ground. "Then I opened the jar and let the mermaid go."

He looked up at the lake as if he was watching the mermaid's body float away. A look of calm came over his face.

I watched him and then the waves as they sloshed onto the beach.

"What happened next?" I asked.

"I fell asleep," said Alvin.

whale fish

sharp tooth

jolly speeder

school of mermaids

The most exotic mermaids
from Alvin's collection.

Kappa
from Japan

Jengu
from Cameroon

My eyebrows rose "You
fell asleep?"
"Yes, right here on the beach."
He pointed again, and we sat
down on the soft moss. I
brushed it with my fingers.
Guilbert copied me. "Hard to
imagine it all dried up and
crusty, isn't it?"
I nodded.
"That's how it was that day
when I fell asleep, but when
I woke up, it had begun to

revive. That's when I knew how
to save the mermaids." He
smiled and jumped up. I
followed as we ran back into
his laboratory
"I came in and grabbed more
specimens," he pointed out the
window, "then I ran out and
threw them into the lake. It took
about an hour to dump them
all and by then I could tell
things were already improving.
I kept back the specimens

Two-tailed siren from Southern Italy

Vodyanoi from Eastonia

from other parts of the world so I could return them."

"What about the mermaids in Lake Nymphette?"

"I went to the airport and chartered a plane. I told them to charge it to the professor's account and they did." He grinned at me. "I arrived back at the lake before the tanker trucks did. As soon as I got to the lab, I grabbed a cart and piled specimens

into it. The lab assistants were used to me. No one questioned what I was doing." He sat back down in his seat looking smug.

I sat down too. "What happened when the trucks arrived?"

"I intercepted them. The drivers knew me and followed my directions to the lake. Then I set the mermaids free."

I couldn't help feeling satisfied as I listened to Alvin. "What happened next?"

"By the time Pearl, the professor and the reporters arrived I was opening the last tank That was good luck because they tried to stop me then. But, I'd learned a few things about reporters and I did something they couldn't resist." He smiled and shrugged. "I made a scene."

I grinned back. "Is that when you went wild?"

He nodded, "The headlines did call me a wild man I started jumping around and shouting "The mermaids

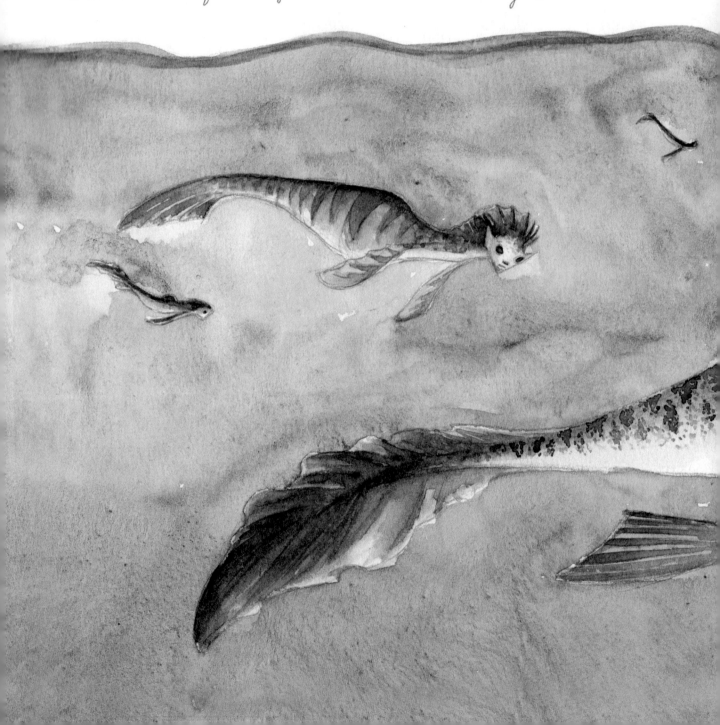

are saved! The mermaids are saved!' I tried to prove it by showing them the moss, but it hadn't been long enough to see evidence of my work. The professor yelled for security, yelled at me, and yelled for security some more 'I'll take your whole collection and your reputation.' He kept saying. He had no idea I'd thrown my collection into the lake! I kept shouting about the mermaids and flailing my arms. It took four or five men to wrestle me into the police car."

Free mermaids
of Lake Nymphette

Lake Horse

Lake Horse

Lake Horse

"You were arrested?"

"Yes, my first and hopefully last time. I spent the night and half the next day in a jail cell. I had no way of knowing what was happening. Had I done enough to save the mermaids?"

"What did the professor do when he learned you threw his collection in the lake?"

"I heard he threw a fit. Luckily by then the moss was beginning to show signs of revival, and the press caught on. After multiple reports of dying mermaids they wanted a happy ending."

"And the professor?"

"Lucky for me the professor had to pretend he wanted to save the mermaids all along. Instead of making my life miserable he refused to press charges. He even gave me an award. The press loved it" He paused and fished around in his desk until he found another newspaper clipping

I took it and began to read.

GUILBERT, Alvin

City of Lake Nymphetto police

Small Droid
Jan 13 1934

TRUTH AND LIBERTY.

LAKE TOWN MONTANA   FOURTEE

FRIDAY   APRIL 30, 1937

MERMAIDS SAVED!

THANKS TO PROFESSOR FOLEY AND HIS TEAM OF SCIENTISTS

Professor Foley and head scientist, Alvin Guilbert had a breakthrough this week. They've saved the mermaids of Lake Nymphette.

"No one could be more pleased than me," said Foley. "This is why we've worked so hard. Guilbert has made a tremendous discovery."

What was Guilbert's fantastic discovery you ask?

"The moss is an important part of the mermaid life cycle. And, it requires nutrients from mermaid remains to keep it alive. We returned many of our specimens to the lake and have had tremendous results," says Guilbert. "We expect the population to revive. In a few years, the lake may recover completely."

Foley presented Guilbert with the first Foley medal. "We want to recognize Guilbert's excellent work." Says Foley, "The award will be an excellent new tradition."

CONTINUED ON PAGE 5

The Foley Medal
Presented to Alvin Guilbert
April 1937

I blinked at the article. "Where's the rest of it?"

Guilbert gave me another shrug. "I didn't save the rest."

I smiled, "but you did save the mermaids."

"Yes, I did."

"What happened to Pearl and the professor?"

Guilbert sighed. "The professor delayed his grand opening. He changed the name of the park to 'Professor Foley's Sea World of Dreams.' It will be a living museum and vacation destination with glass-bottom boat rides. A penny from each ticket sale will go to help save the mermaids around the world. Pearl is still going to be the director."

Lake Semipuella's mermaid population expected to return to normal levels by 1948.

Brown Moss

Reviving Moss

Healthy Moss

mermaid populations
all over the world
have shown promise
of restoration

That didn't seem fair to me. "Don't you feel like Pearl and the professor are getting off too easily?

Alvin Guilbert gave me one last signature shrug. "I got into this mess by trying to control my life, the fate of the mermaids, everything. Things only got better for me when I was willing to let go. I think Pearl and the Professor will get what they deserve. Someday."

"What are your plans now that your a hero?" I asked.

Alvin looked out the window of his barren laboratory. The sun was setting over the lake he loved. "I'm going to keep working to save the mermaids. The difference is, now I know how to do it."

"How is that?"

"By teaching others to follow the rule I should habe followed all along: Don't disturb the mermaids."

THE END

Enjoy 2 Bonus Coloring Pages

•••

Color them in the book or make copies to color again and again.
Keep them for personal use. Don't sell or distribute copyrighted art.

Fish Herder • © Manelle Oliphant 2020

About Manelle

Manelle Oliphant is the illustrator of over ten books for children and the creator of Tales Fantastic, a series of illustrated short stories available free at talesfantastic.com. She lives in Salt Lake City, Utah, with her husband. Learn more about Manelle and her books at talesfantastic.com/artist.

Made in the USA
Coppell, TX
15 July 2020

The younger girls would be swimming to "Let's Go Fly A Kite" from "Mary Poppins". There was also going to be a romantic duet swum by Barbara and Bill, one of the other lifeguards. They would be swimming to "Love Theme from Romeo and Juliet". The show also had a comedy number and two solos.

I was so surprised when Barbara asked me to do a solo.
I was nervous, but immediately said "Yes!" There was
something about synchro that made me so happy, I always
wanted to do more!

A few days later, there was more good news! The pool manager, Nick, told everyone there was going to be a fashion show the same day as the water show. My older sister, Lisa, and her friends were going to be the models. This was becoming an exciting summer for the whole family!

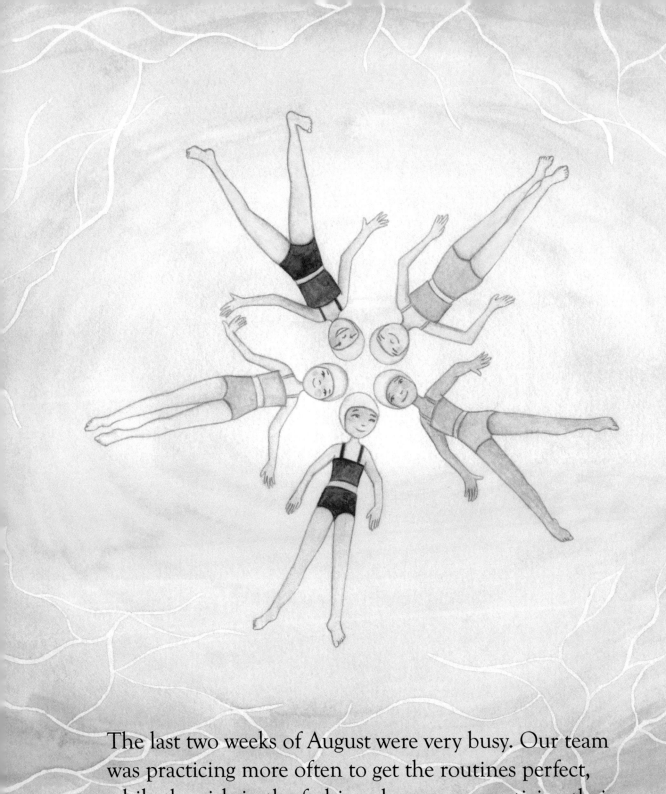

The last two weeks of August were very busy. Our team was practicing more often to get the routines perfect, while the girls in the fashion show were practicing their runway walk.

The shows were scheduled for the last Sunday of the summer. While we were busy practicing, my mother and Barbara were busy sewing our costumes.

There was excitement in the air at our house as the show day got closer. Michele and I watched happily as our mom sewed. The minute she finished, Michele put her costume on. It was perfect!

Finally, the Big Day was here! As we drove, I was excited and nervous at the same time.

Then, I saw the crowded parking lot, and got more nervous. What was I thinking? I was the shy, middle sister. Why did I agree to do a solo?

As soon as we arrived, Lisa, Michele, and I dashed to the ladies room. Inside, there was lots of excitement!

The fashion show was first. The models walked around the pool, while spectators clapped and took pictures. Lisa was the second model and did a great job!

Then it was time for the water show! The Raindrops number was first. We came down the stairs from the sundeck, twirling our umbrellas and dancing to the music. In the pool, we swam in patterns, did ballet legs, and finished with a splashy circle. The audience loved it and we all felt like SUPERSTARS!

Michele and Tina's number was second, followed by the romantic duet, the comedy number, and one of the solos. All of the numbers went well and then it was time for the last routine ~ MY SOLO!!!

As I began my routine on the pool deck, I felt everyone's eyes on me.

I remember thinking ~ THIS IS SCARY ~ but I didn't let that feeling bother me. I told myself to just listen to the music and do my routine, and that's what I did!

When the music ended, there was lots of applause, and I was glad I made it to the end.

As I got out of the pool, people were saying wonderful things to me. My favorite compliment was "I didn't know you were so graceful!"

I was so happy, I couldn't stop smiling! I felt like I was floating on air the rest of the day.

Later that night, my mother said, "Did you have fun today, Wendy?"
"I SURE DID! Swimming SYNCHRO makes me feel good about myself," I answered. "That's called SELF-CONFIDENCE," mother said.

"I LIKE SELF-CONFIDENCE, and I LOVE SYNCHRO! I think I'll be doing SYNCHRO for a long time!!!"

Actually, Wendy Willow is me, Diane Garcia, the author of this book. I did exactly what I told my mother that night. I swam SYNCHRO five more years at the swim club, then in college, and many years after that. I am still swimming SYNCHRO today, making new SYNCHRO friends, and ...LOVING EVERY MINUTE OF IT!!!!

If you like my story and want to be a "water ballerina", you can learn how to get started in the note to your parents at the beginning of this book!

Parents and children can email Wendy Willow (Diane) if you want to chat about synchro or tell her about a synchro team you found, at wendywillow23@si.rr.com.

HAPPY SWIMMING!!!

About the Author

Diane Garcia is a retired teacher living in Staten Island, NY. In addition to her passion for synchronized swimming, she enjoys spending time with her friends and traveling with her husband.

About the Illustrator

Ida Noelle Calumpang is an illustrator and swimmer who discovered her passion for the arts and the aquatics at a very young age. She started speed swimming at the age of seven and went on to become a synchronized swimmer and coach by the time she reached university. Her love of water influences her art where she explores worlds of whimsy and nature, while her artistry has poured into her swimming life where she has worked as a professional mermaid and aquatic performer.

Made in the USA
Coppell, TX
15 July 2020